COOKIE'S WEEK

by Cindy Ward

illustrated by Tomie dePaola

SCHOLASTIC INC.
New York   Toronto   London   Auckland   Sydney

For Paul, who started it all;
for Dr. Eagling and staff, who kept it going;
and, always, for Rodney,
who never turns away a stray. —C W

For all the staff at Russell Animal Hospital,
who like Satie in spite of everything. —T D E P

ISBN 0-590-43604-X
ISBN 0-590-29040-1 (meets NASTA specifications)

Text copyright © 1988 by Cindy Ward.
Illustrations copyright © 1988 by Tomie dePaola.
All rights reserved. Published by Scholastic Inc.,
730 Broadway, New York, NY 10003,
by arrangement with G. P. Putnam's Sons, a division of
the Putnam & Grosset Group.

55 54   7 8 9/0

Printed in the U.S.A.

First Scholastic printing, September 1990

There was water everywhere!

On Tuesday...

Cookie knocked a plant
off the windowsill.

There was dirt everywhere!

On Wednesday...

Cookie upset the trash can.

There was garbage everywhere!

On Thursday...

Cookie got stuck in a kitchen drawer.

There were pots and pans
and dishes everywhere!

On Friday...

Cookie ran into the closet
before the door closed.

There were clothes everywhere!

On Saturday…

Cookie climbed the curtains.

And Cookie *went* everywhere!

Tomorrow is Sunday...

Maybe Cookie will rest!